ONE 1

by

Bill Hunt

Edited by
Lynne North

A CRIMSON SHORT Story

Published by
Crimson Cloak Publishing
All Rights Reserved
Copyright 2015

ISBN 13: 978-1-68160-053-6
ISBN 10: 1-68160-053-6

Table of Contents

CHAPTER ONE

The Gilbert Lumber Company had been around almost as long as the village of Bright itself. The Ohio River town was founded in 1880 and Elias Gilbert opened his lumber yard there in 1885. The steel industry had come to not-too-distant Pittsburgh in 1875, and a steady influx of immigrant steel workers allowed Elias' business to thrive as those workers built houses and put down roots in the area.

By 1945, Bright's population had swelled to 3,500. The town boasted a small, but thriving, business district complete with a bank, several shops and two grocery stores. There were also gas stations at both the north and south ends of the town. But the largest in-town business was Gilbert Lumber.

Then, during the 1980s, the steel industry collapsed. The mills closed as companies sent work overseas where production costs (and labor) were cheaper. The town of Bright seemed to dry up overnight. The shops closed, as did both grocery stores. The north-end gas station went out of business. The town's population plummeted from 3,500 to 1,200. State officials took notice of this and, in 1993, downgraded Bright's status from that of "Town" to "Village."

Yet, through it all, Gilbert Lumber somehow managed not only to survive, but flourish. More than a century of quality products and excellent service had gained them a long list of loyal customers.

The business was now headed by Danny Gilbert, number five in the list of family owners dating back to Elias. He was a tall man (6 foot, 2 inches), powerfully built with slightly thinning sandy-blond hair that belied his relatively young age of thirty five. Danny had married his high school sweetheart, Diane, and together they were raising two boys: Devin, age twelve and Derek, age ten. During the summer months, Danny coached his boys' Little League team, which Gilbert Lumber also sponsored.

Old Elias Gilbert would have been proud of the way his business had grown over the generations. His original store had been little more than a ramshackle shed with a small barn behind it to store lumber. In the 1920s his son, Everett, built the structure that stood now. It was an impressive wooden building, nearly two hundred feet long and one hundred feet wide. The north end of the building contained an office and showroom. This was a spacious area, about fifty feet long and fifty feet wide. Large plate-glass windows gave the people of Bright the opportunity to view the latest offerings as they drove past on the main street through the village. In the early days, Elias had cut his own lumber: nowadays, the wood was delivered via rail. Twice a week, a boxcar laden with wood eased up to the large loading bay on the west side of the building. When the bay doors were closed villagers were treated to a mural of Elias' original store, painted there by a local artist.

One of the many things that endeared Gilbert Lumber to the community was its dedication to tradition. A handshake sealed a deal as firmly as a written contract. Orders were hand-written (and stored on computers later); and a customer in an emergency could get what he needed—even after hours —simply by calling Danny Gilbert at his home.

It was a tradition, in fact, that caused the great disaster.

Back in 1964, Danny's mother, Peg had purchased an artificial Christmas tree to display in the showroom. Not just any artificial tree, mind you: this was a six-foot, silver, aluminum tree in a rotating stand. The tree was decorated with dark-blue ornaments and illuminated by a rotating color wheel which was positioned on the floor about six feet from the tree. As the wheel rotated, a spotlight bathed the tree in ever-changing colors of red, orange, blue and green.

"That is the most hideous looking thing I have ever seen!" bellowed Peg's husband Bob when he saw the tree in the showroom window. "I want it out of my showroom! Take it down and put up something a normal person would want to look at!" Peg, of course, argued to keep the tree: and Peg always won when she and Bob argued. The tree stayed. And it went up year after year - long after everyone else had abandoned the use of silver trees.

Curiously, the people of Bright didn't mind the gaudy little tree. There was something comforting about driving past the lumber company at any time of night between Thanksgiving and Christmas and seeing it shine from the otherwise darkened window: the aging color wheel bathing it in continuously-changing hues of red, orange, blue and green.

CHAPTER TWO

The Bright Methodist Church stood opposite the Gilbert Lumber Company, across the railroad tracks and the paved two-lane road that served as the village's main street. It was a beautiful, two story, gray stone structure built in the early 1900s complete with stained-glass windows and a bell tower.

The church was the home congregation of the Gilbert family. On this night it was also the location of the combined community Christmas Eve Service. (Actually, only the three Protestant churches were combining; the Catholics had been invited, but they respectfully declined, opting instead to stick to their tradition of Midnight Mass.)

Danny Gilbert and family arrived twenty minutes before the 8:00 pm service. They found their usual seats (left-hand side, seven rows back) and settled in. Danny and Diane began to talk quietly to a couple in the pew in front of them while Devin and Derek immediately began to fidget.

Services at Bright Methodist were usually casual-dress affairs, but Diane insisted that Christmas Eve was a "dress up" event. Both boys were in uncomfortably tight dark blue suits, white shirts and ties. Ten year old Derek was a little better off than his brother: his tie was a clip-on. Devin, however, was saddled with the real thing, and his mother had cinched up the knot very tight against his neck. Every few minutes he inserted a couple of fingers between his neck and the collar in an effort to breathe a little easier.

It wasn't merely the occasion of Christmas Eve that prompted Diane to dress up her sons: they were each to have a part in the service and she wanted them to look nice. This did not sit well with the boys, who hated being in front of crowds almost as much as they hated dressing up.

"Why do we have to do this?" Derek had moaned earlier in the evening as his mother clipped on his tie. "Everybody knows the Christmas story and if they don't, they can look it up themselves! They don't need a bunch of kids reciting it for them."

Diane had frowned. "Everyone loves it when kids do Christmas programs. And it isn't like you are going to be reciting alone: a lot of your friends are going to be doing this with you."

"But, not at the same time," Derek had whined. "The preacher is having us go up one at a time to recite our lines! At practice the other day, Brad really blew his line. What if I screw up like he did?"

"I'm sure he didn't mess it up too badly," Diane said soothingly.

Derek rolled his eyes. "Mom, he was supposed to say, 'And she brought forth her firstborn Son and wrapped Him in swaddling clothes and laid Him in a manger.' What he said was, 'And she brought forth her firstborn Son and wrapped Him in a manger and laid Him in a blender!'"

"You're making that up!" Diane said, reprovingly.

"I am not!" Derek countered. "He said it, just like that! People laughed for five minutes and kids made fun of him for the rest of practice! What if I mess up, too?"

"Just calm down," Diane said firmly. "Recite your line for me, just to make sure you have it."

Derek took a deep breath, closed his eyes and said, "And suddenly there was with the angel

a multitude of the heavenly host praising God and saying, 'Glory to God in the highest, and on earth, peace, goodwill towards men.'"

"That's my boy!" Diane had said, giving him a kiss on the cheek. "You are going to do just fine."

Derek shook his head at the memory and leaned back heavily into the pew. Turning to Devin he asked, "When do we go on?"

Devin glanced at the program in his hand. "Not for a while yet. There's going to be some singing, then the preacher is going to talk, then we go on."

Derek sighed audibly. "This is going to be a long night," he groaned.

CHAPTER THREE

Not everyone in the village of Bright was in church that Christmas Eve. Some people had to work. Frank Fluharty was one such person. Frank had worked for the railroad more than fifteen years. He'd started working in the yard, inspecting the rail cars to make certain their brakes and other parts were in order. He'd worked his way up through the ranks and was now an engineer. His route covered a stretch of track from the George's Crossing yard (five miles north of Bright) to Martin's Landing. His primary responsibility was to deliver rail cars full of coal to a power generating plant two miles south of Bright.

Frank was a bachelor and, with no children of his own, regularly took the holiday shift to allow his married co-workers the chance to be with their families. Usually, Frank had a brakeman working with him but, because of the holiday, he was making tonight's seven mile one-way trip by himself.

Tonight's train consisted of an engine and 35 cars filled with coal. The seven mile trip would take a little over 35 minutes. There were two main lines leading south out of the George's Crossing yard: one turned off to the left and offered a direct path to Martin's landing. The other veered to the right and went through Bright to the power plant. The track through Bright was old and the speed limit had been reduced to ten miles an hour. Frank would be detained at the plant for several hours. Each car had to be moved into position on a special platform which held the car in place, and then tipped it upside down to dump its multiple tons of coal. It would be at least seven hours before he would return to the yard.

Frank stepped into the cab promptly at 8:15 pm and began a routine check of valves and gauges.

Everything was in order so, a little past 8:20, he sounded his horn and slowly began to move the train out of the George's Crossing yard towards the village.

CHAPTER FOUR

Back at the Gilbert Lumber Company all was quiet. But, all was not well. The color wheel continued to turn, but the ancient gears of its mechanism were wearing out. The decay was subtle, you could not see it with the naked eye. But, had you been in the empty showroom, you possibly could have noticed a change in sound. Normally, the color wheel emitted a barely audible hum. Over the last few hours however, the hum had grown noticeably louder. And, if you were paying attention, you would have noticed the speed of the wheel had decreased, as if the mechanism was having trouble turning. Indeed, this was the case.

In more modern electrical devices, safeguards have been installed so that when troubles arise, the device shuts off. This is called a "kill" switch.

The color wheel had no such switch. The faltering gears sought to stop the machine, but its shaft kept spinning. The motor began to heat up. This was not the only problem: the tree was not near an electrical outlet, so an extension cord had been used. It stretched from a back storeroom all the way out to the tree. Unfortunately, the cord was nearly as old as the color wheel and it, too, began to heat to a dangerous level. A little after 8:15, a short occurred, and a small fire began to smolder in the back storeroom of the Gilbert Lumber Company.

As noted earlier, the Gilbert Lumber building had been constructed in the 1920s. More modern businesses were equipped with sprinklers or other fire suppression systems, but not Gilbert Lumber. They had been "grandfathered" in under an old system of laws that did not require such measures. The store did have several hand-operated extinguishers: but no one was in the building to operate them when the fire broke out.

For several minutes the fire struggled to survive. The initial "short" had generated a large flash, but the flame quickly diminished to the size of a single candle on a child's birthday cake. Once or twice, it nearly died out. But eventually it gained a foothold in the decades-old wooden planking and began to slowly creep towards a shelf stocked with several large cans of paint thinner.

Police officer Duffy Flowers was driving past Gilbert Lumber just as the short occurred and the color wheel went dark. Duffy, age sixty, had been a friend of the late Bob Gilbert and remembered how he and Peg had sparred over the aluminum tree. "Well," Duffy chuckled to himself, "Looks like Bob finally got his wish! That artificial tree won't bother him anymore."

Inside the store room, the fire reached a shelf full of paint thinner. Some cardboard boxes at the base of the shelf provided the fuel necessary for the fire to spring fully to life. It blazed up to 2 feet in height and began to lick greedily at the cans. The containers began to swell as the liquid inside them boiled and expanded.

Across the street at the Methodist Church, the Christmas Eve program was in full swing. The opening carols had been sung, the preacher had delivered his brief devotional and the children were now giving their recitations.

"I'm gonna throw up," Derek whispered to his older brother, Devin. "I just know I'm gonna flub my lines. I'm so nervous I'm shaking!"

"Relax," said Devin, "You'll do just fine."

"No I won't," asserted Derek, "I can't stand the thought of being up in front of all these people!"

"Don't look at the people," Devin advised. "Look somewhere else."

"Where?" demanded Derek. "Where am I going to look?"

"Just look down the aisle and out the front door," Devin said.

The front door of the Bright Methodist Church consisted of two glass doors. Through the front of the church, Derek would be able to look directly across the way to his father's store.

"I can do that," he said to Devin.

On stage at that moment were a trio of third grade girls reciting Luke chapter 2 verses

8 through 12 in unison:

8 And there were in the same country shepherds abiding in the field, keeping watch over their flock by night. 9 And, lo, the angel of the Lord came upon them, and the glory of the Lord shone round about them: and they were sore afraid.

10 And the angel said unto them, Fear not: for, behold, I bring you good tidings of great joy, which shall be to all people.11 For unto you is born this day in the city of David a Savior, which is Christ the Lord. 12 And this shall be a sign unto you; Ye shall find the babe wrapped in swaddling clothes, lying in a manger.

"You're on," whispered Devin as he nudged his brother towards the aisle.

"Stop shoving!" Derek hissed as he reluctantly got to his feet. He stepped out into the aisle and shuffled towards the stage. "Why did we have to sit so far back?" he complained to himself. He could feel the gaze of everyone in the room: it was if their eyes were burning holes into the back of his head!

After what seemed like ages, Derek reached the front of the sanctuary and turned. He looked straight ahead, out the door, and across the way to the Gilbert Lumber Company.

"This is cool," he thought to himself, "I can't see the tree, but I can see the glow from the wheel! It's red!"

He began his recitation: "And suddenly there was with the angel ..."

Across the street, several paint thinner cans were on the verge of rupture.

"a multitude of the heavenly host..."

"Why doesn't the color change from red to orange," Derek wondered to himself. "Is the wheel stuck?"

"… praising God and saying ..."

The cans of thinner exploded. Because light travels faster than sound, Derek saw, before anyone in the church heard, the blast that blew out the showroom windows of the Gilbert Lumber Company and set the massive wooden structure ablaze.

"DUCK!" Derek screamed.

A thunderous shock wave shook the church. Several women screamed. People were looking around, frantically trying to locate the source of the explosion. Derek pointed towards the door and screamed, "Dad! The lumber yard is on fire!"

The problem with any written account is that events occur much faster than the reader can comprehend. Additionally, many things occur simultaneously. While what follows may take some time to read, all of these things happened within seconds of each other.

At the time of the blast, Frank Fluharty's train was just approaching the third railroad crossing in Bright. It was the only crossing in town with caution lights. It was also the only crossing on the main road through town. The crossing was about 300 yards from the lumber company.

Frank had just sounded the usual warning toot of the locomotive's horn when a huge fireball erupted ahead of him. He quickly applied the brakes, but even at ten miles an hour, a train cannot stop on a dime. The train traveled another 100 feet before it lurched to a stop. Frank noticed some burning material ahead on the track but, because of the thick smoke, he could not determine if the tracks were fully blocked or not. At any rate, it did not seem wise to proceed.

Inside the Methodist Church, several men began a frantic rush for the front and side exits.

They were members of the Bright Volunteer Fire Department.

Bright, like many small, impoverished communities, could not afford a paid fire department. It depended on volunteers. These men held regular jobs, but turned out for fires and other emergencies as the need arose. Also, Bright's firemen relied, not on a radio dispatcher, but a siren system to summon them to duty. Bright had three such sirens positioned throughout the village. Two of them were small 1.5 horsepower devices. Although tiny, the pint-sized sirens emitted a scream that could wake a fireman from the deepest sleep. The third siren was a five horsepower behemoth perched atop a tall tower in the center of town near the little league field. When it went off during a game, all action stopped as players and spectators covered their ears to guard against its shrieking wail.

No 911 phone system was employed in Bright, either. A phone number with the local exchange rang into the control room of the electrical power plant south of the village. There, a plant worker would take the information, mash the button that started the sirens and then wait on the line until someone at the firehouse picked up the phone. The plant worker would then relay the nature and location of the emergency.

On this night over 80% of the firemen immediately knew where the fire was. Still, within 45 seconds of the explosion, Bright's three sirens began to scream.

Those screams were matched by several small children inside the church. The explosion alone had been unnerving; the hustle of the exiting firemen did not help. And, since the lumber yard was less than 50 yards away, the heat from the fire and the smell of smoke created a real sense of imminent danger.

Danny Gilbert was dazed, but only for a moment.

"Diane, take the boys and get out of here! I'm going to see what I can do!"

Diane grabbed her husband's arm in fear. "Danny, don't you dare try to go into that building!"

Danny shook his head, "I won't. But I need to be over there when the firemen get there. I know where all the really flammable stuff is. I don't want anyone getting hurt!" Danny gave his wife a quick kiss and sprinted out the front door.

Diane quickly gathered her sons together. "Come on, boys," she said.

"Where are we going?" asked Devin, concern evident in his voice.

"Just get to the car," his mother said, "We'll figure that out when we get there.

Diane led the boys up onto the church's stage and through a doorway. The door led to a hallway and a rear exit from the church. When they reached the parking lot, the trio turned around. They could not see the lumber company, as it was blocked by the 2-story church building. But a deep red glow hung over the church like a hellish halo.

People were running, children were crying, sirens were screaming, embers were falling.

And the real difficulties were only beginning.

CHAPTER FIVE

Jim Denart was one of the first firemen out of the church. At 48 years of age Jim had been a volunteer for many years and currently served as the department's chief. One look at the blaze let him know that this fire was going to require the assistance of every department in the area. Jim had arrived late for the service and had not parked in the lot, choosing instead to park just off the side of the road, in front of the church, facing south.

The firehouse was at the north end of town. Jim jumped into the front seat of his pickup and switched on the engine. He gunned the motor, did a U-turn ... and immediately noticed that there was a stopped train blocking the main road to the fire house.

Fortunately, just before the crossing, a narrow road branched off to the left. This was High Street. Denart roared up High, praying out loud, "Please, God, don't let that be a unit train!" A unit train was the term given to a regular shipment of coal for the power plant. A unit train consisted of as many as 150 cars. A stopped train of that size would effectively block all firemen from reaching the firehouse.

One block up High Street, Denart came to Smithfield Street. A right turn on Smithfield led directly to the firehouse. Jim was about to make the turn when he saw stopped coal cars. Blocked again!

Denart continued to speed up High. Now he was headed up a steep grade. This was his last hope: at the top of the hill the asphalt intersected with Climb Road. A right turn on Climb would descend back in a sweeping arc towards town - and to the crossing that held Jim Denart's last hope of reaching the fire station.

Denart reached the top of High Street, quickly glanced both ways, and spun the wheel right. As he sped down the hill he noticed that the crossing was clear. His mind raced as he plotted what needed to be done when he reached the firehouse:

1. Call the rail yard and get that train moved!

2. Get his fire crews on their way.

3. Summon help from all available nearby fire departments.

Jim's truck bounced across the tracks at the bottom of the hill. He turned right towards

Bright. A half-mile from the firehouse and a full mile from the fire, he saw the southern sky growing a brighter and brighter red.

"Lord, have mercy," he said to himself, "This is going to be a long night."

CHAPTER SIX

In the cab of his train, Frank Fluharty wrestled with what he should do. A life-long resident of Bright, Frank was horrified to see its best-known landmark in flames. At the same time, he was in a quandary as to what to do with his train. He clearly could not go forward (the initial smoke had cleared and he could now see that a burning power pole, with wires, lay across the track.) He had seen Jim Denart and a host of other firemen head up High Street. He knew that they would have to go all the way to Climb Road in order to access the firehouse. Still, the fire trucks themselves would soon need this crossing at Main Street open if they were to reach the fire. The dilemma? If he reversed the train to open the Main Street crossing too soon, he would cut off firemen at the bottom of Climb Road.

Frank radioed the railroad yard. "This is engine 606! I'm stopped at the Main Street crossing in Bright. The lumber yard is on fire and the track ahead is blocked. I am waiting two, repeat two minutes and then I am returning to the yard!"

A sleepy voice on the radio crackled, "Negative, 606. You need to get that shipment to the plant. Those guys don't want to work Christmas Eve as it is. They aren't going to be happy if you don't show up!"

Fluharty was irked. He keyed the mic and growled,

"Listen up, Dave! The track is blocked. I have a power pole and wires down. The lumber yard is on fire and they are going to need everything in the county to put it out! They MUST have a way in there. Forget the two minutes - I'm heading back now."

Frank switched the radio off and slammed the locomotive's engine into reverse. With a jolt and a puff of black smoke, the train began moving slowly backwards. At the Climb Road crossing, the last firefighter made it across a scant fifteen seconds before the rear coal car reached the intersection.

At the firehouse, the volunteers began to arrive. There would eventually be forty of them, ranging in age from 18 all the way up to 65. The station housed three aging pumper trucks and an emergency squad. Four bay doors went up in rapid succession as the equipment roared to life. There were more men than there was available space on the vehicles. Chief Denart barked out orders.

"Pork, you and Malcolm take engines 2 and 3. I want four guys on each truck! I have pumper #1. Jeffers, you have the squad. I want two EMTs with you. The rest of you, grab your gear and drive your own vehicles to the scene. Park far enough away to leave room for the other departments to get in. Lee, get on the horn and find me some other departments! Tell Newvale, Dillon, Tiltendon and Yorkshire that I want everyone and everything they can spare. Now, let's get going!"

The men scrambled to their assigned posts and the Bright Volunteer Fire Department roared off into the night.

CHAPTER SEVEN

Danny Gilbert stood helplessly at the side of the road, watching the family business burn.

He didn't venture further than the road: he could see the downed power lines. Besides: what could he do? The heat was intense, and growing more so. The overhead sirens had stopped and he could just now hear the distant sound of the trucks leaving the firehouse.

Danny turned and looked back at the church. Some of the worshipers had remained and they now stood in silent clusters on the sidewalk and on the stone steps of the church, watching the blaze. Danny walked slowly back across the street and joined them.

"I'm sorry, Danny" someone said from the back of the crowd. "We all are," said someone else.

Danny bit his lip, but said nothing.

The fire department began to arrive, Jim Denart's pumper #1 in the lead.

"Someone better tell them about the wires!" shouted someone on the sidewalk.

"They see it," said someone else. "Look!"

The crowd could see Chief Denart holding his men back as he pointed towards the power pole lying across the tracks. The wires extended back to the burning building and, every so often, sparks could be seen. Fortunately, within minutes, a truck from the electric generating plant arrived on scene and cut the power. The firemen then began to move into position to fight the fire.

Now that it was safe, Danny Gilbert jogged across the street. He scrambled down the embankment, crossed the railroad tracks and approached Chief Denart.

"Jim, I want you to know that there's nothing in that building worth risking anybody's life."

"Are there any kind of chemicals or anything in there that we should be worried about?" Denart asked.

Danny looked at the building. "We had some paint thinner and some paint in that first storeroom. It looks like the fire is past that already. All we have left in there now is wood. Lots of it. This could burn for quite a while."

Denart reached for a walkie-talkie that was clipped to his fire coat. "Alright, guys, listen up! We are going to fight this fire defensively. No one goes into the building. We put as much water on it as we can from the outside and let it burn itself out. Do we have an ETA yet on any of those other departments?"

The radio crackled. "This is Tiltendon. We'll have a pumper there in about twenty minutes."

A few moments later the radio came to life again. "This is Newvale. We have a pumper and a tanker about fifteen minutes away."

Yorkshire and Dillon's departments didn't respond , but each of them pulled onto the scene within five minutes. Dillon brought a pumper while Yorkshire, the largest department in the region, sent its ladder truck. The ladder was equipped with a "deluge gun": a special hose system that allowed water to be sprayed down on the fire from a great height.

Chief Denart turned to face Danny. "I know this is rough, but with a little bit of luck, I think we can get a handle on this."

Unfortunately, luck can turn in any number of directions.

CHAPTER EIGHT

"Mom, we can't just sit here!" Derek paced the floor of the living room. Diane, not knowing exactly what to do, had chosen to take her boys home and wait for news from her husband. They had been home now for about 45 minutes.

"Sit down, stupid, you're not helping", groused Devin.

"Leave your brother alone, Devin," said Diane wearily. "I'm sure he's just upset like the rest of us. Your father will call as soon as he knows something."

"What is there to know?" demanded Derek. "His whole world is burning down and we're sitting here doing nothing!"

"Do you want me to stuff him in the closet, Mom?" Devin asked, letting his annoyance show. "I can do it: I've done it before."

"Just stop!" snapped Diane. "Both of you, just knock it off right now! Find something to occupy yourselves. Watch TV if you can't think of anything else!" With that, she stormed off to the kitchen.

"You heard her," said Devin. "Find something on the tube, Dweeb."

Grudgingly, Derek picked up the remote and turned on the television. Sadly, there isn't much in the way of exciting programing after 9:00 pm on Christmas Eve. Several stations were carrying religious services, one cable channel had a marathon showing of a Christmas movie they had seen several times. Eventually, the two of them found themselves watching the Weather Channel.

"My life has hit rock bottom," sighed Derek as he flopped onto the couch.

Suddenly, Devin sat forward in his chair. "Look at the map, bro," he said to Derek. "That's where we live. Why is there a red box around it? Turn up the volume so I can hear what the guy is saying."

Dutifully, Derek increased the sound level.

"If you've been watching with us over the past couple of days," the announcer was saying, "then you know we've been following this storm coming out of the southwest. Earlier in the week it looked like it was going to come right up the coast and be a good old-fashioned Nor'easter. But, over the last day or so it has run into this front and, as a result, it has taken a sharp turn to the northwest. Consequently, people from the mountains of Virginia, all the way up into West Virginia and the Ohio Valley are going to experience a rapid drop in temperature. This is going to be accompanied by strong winds and heavy snow. We are talking snowfall up to eight inches and wind gusts as high as fifty miles an hour from out of the southeast. Stay with us here at the Weather Channel: we'll be coming back to this story right after the break."

Devin frowned. "I don't like the sound of that. Fifty mile-an-hour winds can really whip up a fire. Do you remember when Dad made a campfire in the backyard and that storm came up? Right before the rain started the wind blew really hard: the fire burned for a couple of minutes just like a blowtorch! I think Mom ought to see this." He left for the kitchen and returned with his mother, just as the weather report was being repeated.

"Did you hear that, Mom?" Devin asked. "Fifty mile-an-hour winds could whip that fire up pretty bad!"

"Did he say the winds would be out of the southeast?" Diane asked, turning pale.

"Yeah," said Derek, casually. "So what?"

"It won't just whip the fire up," Diane whispered hoarsely. "It will blow it back on the town!"

CHAPTER NINE

60 year-old Doris Enoch had been sitting with her husband, Drew, on the right-hand side of the Methodist Church when the Gilbert Lumber Company erupted into flame. The blast shook, but did not break, the large stained-glass window her parents had donated to the church when she was a small child. Drew joined the rest of the firemen in their mad dash for the firehouse. Doris, however, remained at the church. Once she saw the size of the fire, she quickly scanned the dwindling number of worshipers for other members of the Firemen's Auxiliary. The Auxiliary was made up of women: wives of the fire-fighters, mostly, whose main function was to staff the food tent at the annual Street Fair. On rare occasions, such as when there was a large fire, the Auxiliary would prepare coffee, sandwiches and other food for battle-weary firemen.

This was clearly one of those occasions.

Quickly, Doris rounded up five of the other older Auxiliary members. "We're going to need more help than this," she said, with disappointment in her voice. "There will be more than 100 firefighters on this fire."

"Who are we going to get?" asked Edna McGuire. "We're a bunch of empty-nesters: all the other members have kids at home!"

"I don't care," Doris said, bluntly. "We need everybody, or

at least as many as we can get. Call Shawna Davis. She is secretary at the Presbyterian Church. They have a nice youth facility. Tell her that we are going to have the Auxiliary members drop their kids off there."

"Now, wait a minute," Edna began, but Doris cut her off.

"Do it!"

Meekly, Edna went off to make the call. Doris turned her attention to the remaining members.

"What supplies do we have in the firehouse kitchen?" she demanded.

"We have a couple of pounds of coffee, some tea and a bunch of hot chocolate packets," said June Shields.

"What about food?" Doris asked.

"No food," replied June, flatly.

"I hate living in a town with no store," Doris muttered.

"It wouldn't matter if we did have a store," June reminded her. "It's Christmas Eve."

"Well, we have to feed those men something!" Doris barked. "Alright, when we call the other Auxiliary members tell them to go through their refrigerators and cupboards and bring whatever they can: soup, sandwich fixings, chips— anything they can lay their hands on. I want you girls to swing by your houses and do the same. Then, get to the firehouse as soon as you can: I want everyone there within the hour."

The ladies dispersed without saying a word: you didn't argue with Doris.

CHAPTER TEN

"Hurry up, boys!" Diane shouted. "Get changed. Put on your warmest clothes, your coats, hats and gloves and get out to the car! I'm going to try to call your father!" Diane's hands shook as she pushed the buttons on her cell phone. She pressed the phone to her ear. "He's not answering! Why isn't he answering!?" After a few moments more, Diane threw the phone into her purse, put on her warm clothing and joined her sons in the car.

"Where are we going?" Derek asked.

"We have to tell your father about the storm. They may already know, but they might not!" Diane slammed the car into gear and roared out of the driveway. The Gilbert home was located at the south end of Bright, almost a mile from the lumber yard. The red glow from the fire was still clearly visible, although Diane could also detect clouds of steam as the hoses poured thousands of gallons of water onto the blaze.

Just then, Diane's phone emitted a piercing tone: it was the Emergency Broadcast signal. She threw the phone into the back seat.

"What does it say?" she asked, panic in her voice.

Devin read the text message: " 'High Wind Warning for your area from 11:00 pm till 4:00 am.

Sustained winds out of the southeast at forty miles per

hour with gusts up to 60'. Sixty? The Weather Channel said it would only be up to fifty!"

By this time, Diane had made the left turn onto the main road that would take her to the lumber company. She was forced to stop several hundred yards from the scene, however: by carloads of spectators who had turned out to stare at the blaze. They completely blocked the street. It was impossible to get through.

Diane pulled over to the side of the road and they all got out.

Diane turned to her sons. "Boys," she said, "your father is not answering his phone. I don't know if anybody down there knows about the storm that's coming. I need you two to get down there and tell somebody!"

"How do we do that?" Derek asked.

"I know!" shouted Devin. "We can go down over the embankment here and run up the tracks!"

At that moment, a brief, but very strong gust of wind struck them full in the face.

"Get going!" Diane shouted.

The boys scampered down the embankment and onto the tracks. They hurried as fast as they dared run, being careful not to trip on the railroad ties. Within minutes they reached their father, who was standing by Pumper #1 with Chief Denart.

"What are you two doing here?" demanded Danny.

"There's a storm coming," panted Devin. "Forty mile an hour sustained winds with gusts up to sixty." He gulped hard to catch his breath before blurting out, "High wind warning is in effect from 11 pm to 4 am. It's going to be coming out of the southeast." Almost as an afterthought, he added, "We're supposed to get heavy snow after that."

Denart spat out a profanity. "That's just what we need," he growled. He looked at the fire, then swung his gaze back to the Methodist Church and the bunched row of two-story wooden houses that flanked it on the left and right. He reached for his fire radio.

"Attention all units! We have a high-wind warning going into effect in less than an hour. It will last for five hours and it is going to be coming out of the southeast. I want Tiltendon, Newvale and Dillon to cease pumping and move your engines up onto the main road. Bright and Yorkshire, continue to fight the lumber fire." Denart paused a moment before keying the microphone again. "Bright Fire Command calling Bright Police department. Are you there, Duffy?"

There was no answer. He repeated the message, but there was still no reply.

Jim Denart turned to the Gilbert boys. "Do you know Officer Flowers?"

"Yes, sir," answered Devin.

"You and your brother go find him," the Chief said, "and tell him to call me on the radio immediately."

"Yes, sir!" both boys answered in unison, before racing off.

"What do you need Duffy for?" asked Danny Gilbert.

Jim Denart looked grim as he gestured towards the houses. "I want those homes evacuated."

"Why?" asked Danny, in surprise. "It looks like the lumber yard is almost under control."

Denart shook his head. "It won't be once the wind hits it. At any rate, I don't want to take a chance. Those houses over there are not only made out of wood: they're old. They don't have any of the modern fire-breaks in them. I'm most worried about a roof fire, but a fire anywhere on the structure could spread pretty rapidly. On top of that, look how close the houses are: there's barely fifteen feet between them."

As if to emphasize his point, at just that moment, a gust of wind sent a shower of sparks from the lumber yard high into the night sky.

"How many houses are you going to evacuate?" Danny asked.

Chief Denart didn't hesitate. "Two blocks wide in each direction and two blocks deep."

Danny gasped. "You've got to be kidding," he said. "You're talking about a quarter of the town! Where will everyone go?"

Jim Denart shrugged. "That's Duffy's problem," he said. "I've got a fire to fight."

CHAPTER ELEVEN

Doris Enoch waded through the crowded firehouse kitchen, carefully maneuvering around people, pots and an ever-increasing amount of food. The kitchen was large enough to comfortably accommodate six workers under normal conditions but, at the moment, nearly a dozen women vied for workspace while another fifteen stood in the dining area impatiently awaiting instructions. Doris grabbed a large stew pot with her left hand and a long-handled ladle with her right. She began banging the two together, creating an awful racket. Everyone stopped what they were doing and stared at her. When the room was completely quiet, she spoke.

"Ladies," she began, "I can't tell you how much I appreciate your willingness to help, but we have GOT to get organized!" She looked at the clock on the kitchen wall. "It is now 9:45. The men have been fighting the fire for almost an hour and a half. This is going to be an all-night affair. I want to have soup and sandwiches ready to go by 11:00 pm. The first order of business, however, is hot drinks! I want coffee and hot chocolate ready to go ASAP!" She pointed to a woman with salt-and-pepper hair. "Karen! You and Elaine get to work on that right away! Now, what do we have in the way of soups?"

Anna Patrino shouted, "I've got a huge pot of Italian Wedding Soup. We had family coming in tomorrow for Christmas. I have enough to feed about twenty people."

"I was expecting as many people as Anna," hollered Debbie Berzelli. "I've got vegetable soup for about twenty."

"That's still only half of what we need," Doris said, grimly. "Did anybody bring any chicken?"

Several women shouted that they had brought turkey.

"That'll do," Doris said, decisively. "Get all of the meat off of one of the smaller birds and cube it up for soup. Slice the rest of the turkey up for sandwiches. We've got plenty of vegetables to chop up. Did anyone think to bring any packets of noodles?"

"I have two large bags of mini, frozen egg noodles right here," called Valerie Tiffing.

"They go with the soup," Doris directed. "Now, what do we have in the way of sweets? Those guys could use a little instant energy."

That was probably the easiest food problem to solve: Nearly every Auxiliary member had brought bags, boxes or plastic containers of Christmas cookies with them.

The hot drinks left the station at 10:30 and, remarkably, the rest of the food was on scene by Doris' 11:00 pm deadline.

CHAPTER TWELVE

The Gilbert boys did not take long finding Officer Duffy Flowers. They knew that they had not seen his police cruiser when they were on the way to the fire, so they began their search in front of the Methodist Church and then ran north. They found the patrolman at the Main Street rail crossing, diverting traffic onto High Street, away from the fire area.

"Officer Flowers," huffed an out of breath Devin, "Chief Denart has been trying to reach you on your radio."

Wordlessly, Duffy turned and trotted to his police car, which was blocking Main Street about 20 feet away. He reached through the open driver's side door and picked up the microphone.

"This is Officer Flowers. Come in, Chief Denart."

Jim Denart responded immediately. "This is Chief Denart. Go ahead, Duffy."

"What was it you wanted, Jim?" Flowers asked.

"I need you to evacuate a bunch of houses, Duffy."

Flowers was shocked. "What the heck for, Jim? I thought you guys had things under control."

The irritation was evident in Denart's response: "We HAVE the fire under control, for now,

Duffy. The problem is that we have a storm coming in

from the southeast with sustained winds of 40 miles an hour and gusts up to 60. Do you see the problem?"

Flowers looked back towards the fire, a little less than a quarter of a mile away, for just a moment before he answered. "Yeah. I see the problem. How large of an area do you want to evacuate?"

Chief Denart's voice crackled over the radio. "I want everything from the Main Street rail crossing all the way down to two blocks past the Methodist Church. Two blocks deep."

Flowers gave a low whistle. "That's a lot of people, Jim. Can you spare any men to help me knock on doors?"

"Negative," answered the Chief. "I'm in the process of moving some trucks up onto Main Street right now just in case we get some embers blowing over that way. I need everybody else down here on the lumber yard fire. You're going to have to find some help on your own."

Duffy tossed the microphone onto the driver's seat and walked back to the Gilbert boys. "I'm drafting you two to help me with a problem," he said. "We have to evacuate a bunch of houses. I'll show you which ones have to be cleared. I want you to knock on doors and tell the occupants to evacuate to either firehouse if they are above the Methodist Church, or the high school if they live below the Methodist Church. Got it?"

The boys stared blankly at Duffy for a couple of seconds before Derek asked, "Why would people leave their houses just because a couple of kids told them to?"

Flowers strode briskly back to his cruiser and returned a moment later with a police walkie-talkie. He handed it to Devin. "If anyone gives you any guff, show them this. It is an official police radio: it even has the department name and logo on it. Tell them if they don't evacuate, you are going to radio me and that Officer Duffy Flowers is going to haul their butt off to jail! Is that clear?"

"Yes, sir!" both boys shouted in unison.

"Good," said Duffy with a wink and a grin. "Now, get going. Chief Denart wants those houses evacuated as quickly as possible. Tell people not to waste time gathering possessions. They can take some pillows and blankets with them, but tell them that they will most likely be sleeping on the floor."

The boys nodded and raced off on their errand. Surprisingly, they met with very little resistance. A few residents had to be prodded with Officer Flowers' threat of jail, but most were eager to comply with the evacuation order. The wind had grown steadily stronger since 11:00 pm, and a number of residents had become increasingly alarmed by the embers that blew high into the night—and ever closer to their homes.

By 11:45 the boys were almost to the Methodist Church. In fact, only one house stood between them and the old, stone church. That house, a massive two-story wooden structure, belonged to an elderly widow by the name of Edna Householder. Edna's late husband, Earl, had been a carpenter. When he was alive, the Householder home had been one of the most beautiful houses in Bright. But Earl had been dead for almost 25 years now, and the house and yard had fallen into disrepair. Some friendly neighbors regularly helped with the lawn, but the house clearly showed the ravages of time: the paint was peeling, roof shingles were missing, and the attic window facing Main Street was broken. Pigeons could regularly be seen flying in and out of the building. Edna was now something of a recluse, living quietly in her decaying home with two cats: Tink and Bella.

The Gilbert boys knocked on the back door several times before Mrs. Householder opened it an inch or two and asked what they wanted.

"We're sorry, ma'am," Devin replied, "but the fire chief has ordered an evacuation of all the houses near the fire. You are supposed to take a blanket and pillow and go to either the high school or the fire house."

"I'm not going anywhere," Mrs. Householder said firmly. She started to close the door.

"Wait!" shouted Derek. "Officer Flowers gave us this police radio. He said if anyone refused to evacuate we were supposed to call him and he would take them to jail!"

Edna Householder opened the door a little further and pointed a bony finger at the boys. "You tell that scrawny little sawed-off twerp to mind his own business and leave me alone!"

With that, she slammed the door in the face of the Gilbert boys.

"What do we do now?" Derek asked, turning to his brother.

Devin shrugged. "I guess we call Officer Flowers. Let me have the radio."

Derek handed the device to his older brother and Devin pressed the microphone button. "Officer Flowers? Are you there?"

A moment later, the radio crackled. "This is Officer Flowers."

"This is Devin Gilbert. We're at the Householder place and Mrs. Householder won't leave."

An obviously annoyed Buddy Flowers responded, "Tell her that if she doesn't leave, I'm taking her to jail!"

"We told her that," Devin said into the walkie-talkie.

"What did she say?" Flowers demanded.

Devin did not answer.

"I asked you: what did she say?"

Derek grabbed the radio from his brother. "She said that you were a scrawny little, sawed-off twerp and that you should leave her alone!"

Devin snatched the radio back. "Don't say that, stupid!" he hissed at his sibling through clenched teeth.

"I'll be there in a couple of minutes!" an enraged Duffy Flowers bellowed over the radio. Sure enough, in a matter of minutes, the town's police cruiser screeched to a stop in the Householder driveway—blue lights flashing. Duffy emerged from the car, slamming the door behind him, strode briskly to the back door and began pounding on it.

"Edna! This is the police! Open up this instant!"

From behind the closed door, came the muffled reply, "Go away!"

In the pale glow of the back door light, the Gilbert boys could see Duffy's face turn purple with rage. "Open up this door, Edna, or I swear I will knock it down!"

The door opened a few inches and frail Edna Householder glared at the officer. "Duffy Flowers, you were a pain in the butt when I was your teacher and you haven't changed a bit!"

Before Flowers could say a word, Derek blurted, "You were his teacher, Mrs. Householder?"

Edna never took her eyes off the policeman as she nodded in the affirmative. "Seventh grade English," she said. "He was the whiniest little nose-picker in the class! Duffy, don't you have anything better to do than to hassle old ladies at midnight?"

Duffy controlled himself, but just barely. "Doggone it,

Edna! Jim Denart has ordered that a quarter of the town be evacuated. This storm has winds that might blow the fire back on these houses. We don't want to risk anyone getting hurt!"

Mrs. Householder was defiant. "Well, I'm not going anywhere without my cats! I haven't seen either of them since the explosion. They're inside cats, so I know they're in here somewhere. I'm not leaving until I find them, and that's that!"

"Now, listen here, you crazy old woman," Duffy started. But, he was cut off by Devin, who suddenly shouted, "If you leave, Mrs. Householder, Derek and I will find them for you!" (Devin had, at one time, been Edna's paper boy: she knew both Gilbert boys very well).

"What did you say?" Officer Flowers and Edna Householder asked in unison.

Devin repeated, "I said that my brother and I will find your cats if you promise to go to one of the shelters. I have my cell phone with me and Mom is just up the street a couple of blocks. We'll take them to our place until it is safe for you to come home."

Edna pondered the offer for a moment, then opened the door. "Come on in, boys! Buddy, you stay right where you are! I'll get my coat and be out in just a minute!"

She ushered the boys into the house and closed the door on the patrolman.

"I don't know whose bright idea it was to give that moron a badge, but he ought to be slapped silly," Mrs. Householder groused to herself.

"He's just trying to do his job, ma'am," Devin said, apologetically.

The old woman shook her head sadly. "I know," she said, "I'm just worried sick about my cats!"

"Do you have any idea where they might be?" Derek asked.

"I've looked all over the downstairs and can't find them," Mrs. Householder said. "The door to the basement is closed, so they can't be down there. My guess is that they went upstairs. My legs aren't so good so I don't go up the steps myself anymore. My bedroom is down here, just off of the living room."

"We'll find them for you," Devin promised. "Do you have anything we can put them in?"

"I have two little carriers called 'pet taxis' that I use when I take them to the vet's," Mrs. Householder said. "They just happen to be on a shelf in the front hallway. Stay here and I'll get them for you."

Edna returned with the pet carriers in a few moments and handed one to each boy. "You take good care of my kitties," she admonished them. "Now, I'd better get my coat and go outside before Dudley Dooright out there has me arrested!"

In a matter of minutes, the boys were alone in the crumbling house.

The stairs were easy enough to find. The boys had entered the house through the back door. This put them into a small entry way that led into the kitchen. The kitchen led to the dining room, which in turn led to a hallway that took them to the front door.

The stairway was just to the left as you faced the front door.

The boys stood at the bottom of the stairs for a few moments, looking up, before they actually ventured upstairs. Mrs. Householder had kept the bottom floor of her home reasonably clean. But, as she had told the boys, she no longer went upstairs. And, when she cleaned, she apparently only cleaned the stairs that she could comfortably reach with her vacuum. The carpet on the bottom four steps was clean: above that, the boys could see dust, scraps of paper, cat toys and other debris.

Devin located a light switch at the bottom of the stairs and flipped it on. A single, bare bulb began to glow at the top of the stairs.

The stairs near the top were very dirty indeed.

"This ought to be loads of fun," said Derek in a voice that indicated he anticipated having no fun at all. Before heading up the stairs, he turned and looked through the front door window at the lumber yard fire.

"Wow," he said to his brother, Devin. "The wind is really whipping the fire up pretty good."

Indeed, it was. It was now 12:15 am, Christmas Day. The Gilbert Lumber Company had been burning for almost four hours. Eighty percent of the building was already destroyed. The outer walls were gone on the side facing Main Street and the roof had collapsed. Although the fire departments continued to pour water on the blaze, the large stacks of wood were arranged in such a way that water could not reach all of the fire. The sustained winds fanned the flames in these protected areas and blew showers of sparks high into the night sky.

No one, however, noticed the embers that drifted through the broken attic window into the Householder home.

CHAPTER THIRTEEN

"We might as well get this over with," Devin said as he started up the stairs. "Watch your step."

This was good advice: the clutter rapidly increased as the boys neared the top of the sixteen stairs. Along with the debris deposited by the cats, there were paint chips and shreds of wall paper. And dust - lots of dust.

"Look at this mess!" Derek exclaimed. "You would think we would be able to track the cats' footprints in the dirt! Where do you think they went?"

"How should I know?" grumbled Devin. "I've never been in this house before. I always thought it would be cool to go exploring, but this place gives me the creeps. Let's find the cats and get out of here!"

The boys arrived at the top of the stairs. They stood in a small, open area with doors on all four walls around them. Every door, except one, was open. Immediately in front of them, facing the rear of the house, the open door revealed a bathroom that had not been used by humans in years. To the right, two open doors revealed bedrooms. This was also true of the two doors on the left.

"I wonder what that door leads to," Derek asked, pointing to the door on the wall at the front of the house.

"It doesn't matter," Devin said. "That door is closed, so

the cats can't be in there. My guess is that it leads to the attic." (He was right about that.)

"How do you want to do this?" Derek asked. "Do you want to split up? You could take the two rooms on the right and I can look in the rooms on the left."

Devin shook his head. "No, I don't think so. There are two cats: we would stand a better chance of catching them if we each went into a room together, shut the door behind us, and searched it. I can't imagine that either cat is going to like being caught by a stranger. It might help if one of us does the catching and the other one holds the pet carrier open."

Derek nodded in agreement. "Where do you want to start?"

Devin pointed to the wall on his right, to the door closest to the front of the house. "We'll start there. We'll work counter-clockwise until we search each room. You follow me and, whatever you do, don't let either of the cats get past you!"

The boys entered the first bedroom as quietly as they could and closed the door behind them: but not before Devin had located the light switch and turned it on. Again, a single bulb illuminated the room. The room had a large 4-poster double bed in it. The bed had a ruffle around the bottom of it that brushed the floor.

"Get on the floor and look under the bed," Devin commanded.

"Why me?" Derek asked.

"Because I said so," his brother answered.

With a sigh of disgust, Derek flopped to his stomach and peered under the bed.

"See anything?" Devin asked.

"Yeah," Derek replied. "I see the world's largest herd of

dust bunnies! This is nasty!"

"But, no cats?" Devin prodded.

"No cats."

"O.K. That's one room down. Let's move on to the next one," Devin said. "We'll close the door behind us so the cats can't run in here if we flush them out of another room."

The second room on the right had been Edna Householder's sewing room. There were shelves of boxes and bolts of fabric along three of the four walls. The remaining wall was where Edna's ancient, foot-operated Singer sewing machine stood. Again, however, no cats were to be found.

"The bathroom is next," Devin said as he closed the bedroom door behind them.

The cats were not in the bathroom, either. They had, however, been there at some time in the past: all of the toilet paper had been unwound from the roll and was lying in a pile on the floor.

"Only two rooms left," Derek said as they moved to the rear room on the left side of the house. This room was the most cluttered of all: it had been used as a store room and was piled from floor to ceiling with boxes, furniture and a variety of other items.

"This room is full of hiding places," Devin said. "If I were a cat, this is where I would hide."

As it turned out, that is exactly where Tink and Bella had gone to escape the excitement. Catching the two felines proved to be more of a challenge than the Gilberts anticipated: it was a full fifteen minutes before both animals were successfully cornered and crated.

"Man!" said Derek as he leaned against the wall, "I am whipped! I never knew you could get that tired chasing cats!"

"Listen!" Devin said, suddenly, "what's all that noise?"

"What noise?" Derek asked.

"I hear people yelling!" Devin answered. "What are they saying?"

"Who knows?" Derek said casually. "It's probably somebody across the street at the lumber yard."

"Be quiet!" Devin ordered, "I'm trying to hear what they are saying!"

Both boys strained their ears. There seemed to be several people shouting. Much of what was said was undecipherable. Suddenly, though, both boys clearly heard someone shout, "The Householder place is on fire!"

CHAPTER FOURTEEN

Devin Gilbert jerked open the bedroom door just in time to see a large, flaming portion of the second floor ceiling fall, blocking the stairway exit. He ducked back into the bedroom and slammed the door behind him.

"We've got trouble, bro!" he shouted, "the house is on fire!"

Frantically, the boys looked around the room. The only possible escape was through a window which was blocked by a huge pile of boxes. The boys hurriedly threw these out of the way and tried to raise the window.

It would not budge.

"Quick!" Devin shouted, "Give me that chair!" He pointed to a small folding chair that rested against a stack of boxes.

Derek tossed the chair to his older brother.

Devin broke the window glass with the chair and then used it to clean the frame of any shards.

"Come on, Derek!" he commanded. "Get out on the porch roof!"

"Not without the cats," Derek said. "We promised Mrs. Householder."

Wisps of smoke began to filter in around the bedroom

door.

"Bring the stupid cats!" Devin shouted, "but hurry up!"

Derek picked up the two pet carriers and hurried to the window. He set the carriers out on the roof and then scurried out after them. Devin followed close behind.

The back porch roof was only about twelve feet off the ground: a survivable drop under normal circumstances. However, the area under the boys was littered with bricks and other debris.

A sudden blast of heat let the boys know that the fire had entered the bedroom. They moved away from the open window, as close to the edge as they dared go, and screamed for help.

Help was already on the way: members of the Tiltendon Volunteer Fire Department were scrambling up the hill with a ladder. In a matter of minutes, the boys and the cats were safely on the ground. A few moments after that, the boys joined their parents on the town's Main Street.

CHAPTER FIFTEEN

Christmas morning finally dawned on the village of Bright. The wind had died down sooner than expected, around 2:00 am—roughly the same time that the snow started. At daylight, a fresh five inches of snow covered the area. The snow could not, however, conceal the ravages of the night before.

The Gilbert Lumber Company was gone. Not a single shred of the building remained. Although flames were no longer visible, smoke rose from a few charred piles of smoldering ruins.

Edna Householder's home was a shambles as well. The roof and second story were gone. (The rest of the structure would be bulldozed shortly after New Year.)

And there was a third casualty as well: that one was located at the Methodist Church. The Householder residence was only about 15 feet from the church. Firemen were fearful that the flames would spread to it, so they poured water onto the church all the time they were fighting the house fire.

Unfortunately, heat had already built up and, when the first stream of water hit it, Doris Enoch's beloved stained-glass window shattered into a million pieces.

During the night, the four churches in town (Presbyterian, Methodist, Christian and Catholic) had come together, pooled their resources, and organized a breakfast for all of the firemen who had fought so hard to save their town. All of the more than eighty firefighters stayed for the meal, including those from Newvale, Tiltendon, Dillon and Yorkshire. (To be honest, all of them were too tired at that point to make the drive home.)

The breakfast was held in the high school gymnasium.

Nearly every resident of Bright was there. Some brought food, some prepared food, some served food.

A group of firemen was sitting on the gymnasium floor, leaning back and resting themselves against the wall. One of them noticed a little girl, about five years old, walking across the gym floor, crying.

"What's the matter, sweetheart?" one of them asked. "Can't you find your Mommy?"

The little girl shook her head. "No," she said. " My Mom is right over there."

"Then, what's wrong?" the firefighter asked.

The little girl broke into heavy sobs. " It's Christmas morning and Santa Claus didn't come last night! Mom got us out of bed early to come here and there was nothing under the tree!"

The little girl ran off and disappeared into the crowd.

The firefighters looked at each other.

"Cripes!" one of them said. "My kids are going to be upset, too. I know there's nothing under our tree: I was here all night!"

As it turned out, nearly every household in Bright faced the same problem: no presents under the tree on Christmas morning.

"I have an idea," said one of the older firemen.

A few minutes later, David Sindlinger, the mayor of Bright, picked up a microphone and called for everyone's attention. The gymnasium grew quiet.

"On behalf of the people of Bright, "Sindlinger began, "I want to thank all the firemen from all the departments for fighting so hard to protect our town. We lost a lot last night, but it would have been a lot worse if not for your hard work." The mayor's voice cracked with emotion and he had to compose himself before he continued. "They say that in times of tragedy, neighbors help neighbors. I want to thank our neighbors from Newvale, Yorkshire, Dillon and Tiltendon. We owe you a debt of gratitude that we will never be able to repay. And, to the people of Bright, let me just say this: I have never seen a greater expression of friendship than I've witnessed in these last difficult hours. You gave up your comfort and your resources and your time to help your friends. Well done!"

The gymnasium was silent, the moment was too emotional for the cheap formality of applause.

The mayor reached into his shirt pocket and produced a piece of paper. "I have one more announcement to make. This is for all the children. It comes from a good friend of yours. I think you will be able to identify him long before I finish reading."

David Sindlinger cleared his throat and began. "My dear friends: last night I started on my journey, as I do every year, with the intent of spreading joy and happiness to as many people as possible. I arrived at your town a little before midnight and was horrified to see what was happening to it. I must have circled overhead for nearly half-an-hour, watching the bravery of the men who battled both the fire and the elements. I saw the Women's Auxiliary working tirelessly to bring hot food and drink to those noble firemen. And I listened to the phone calls of countless others who worked late into the night planning the breakfast that you so recently enjoyed. Somehow, the thought of coming into your empty homes to leave presents just didn't seem right. I'm sorry if that upset you, my intentions were the best. So, I tell you what I will do: just for you and for the families of the brave volunteers from the surrounding communities - I will return tonight and leave the presents I was so hesitant to drop off last evening. Best wishes on this Christmas Day, your friend, Santa Claus."

EPILOGUE

Life went on in Bright after the big fire: the people there are a hardy lot.

Danny Gilbert announced during the second week of January that Gilbert Lumber would rebuild. "There's no sense in having insurance on your business of you don't plan on using it," he said. "Besides, I don't know how to do anything else!" In a little under a year, he was back in business with all of his old customers (and maybe a few others.)

Edna Householder decided to move to a senior center in the town of Tiltendon. The center did not allow cats, so Tink and Bella went to live with, of all people, Buddy Flowers!

The Gilbert boys patiently worked through the second half of the school year and returned to their real love: Little League baseball (again, sponsored by Gilbert Lumber).

As for Doris Enoch, she did not replace her beloved stained-glass window. "The darn things break!" she complained. Instead, she and her husband donated a bronze plaque which stands at the north entrance to the village of Bright. The plaque reads: "Welcome to Bright: the only town in the world where Santa comes on December 26th - and your friends come whenever you are in trouble!"

THE END

About the Author

Bill Hunt lives in Ohio with his wife Linda, where he has been the minister of the Rosehill Church of Christ in Reynoldsburg since 1992. They have two married daughters.

He is the author of the Garson the Dragon series.

https://www.facebook.com/pages/Garson/1510374865881162
http://www.garsonbooks.com/
On Smashwords
https://www.smashwords.com/books/view/488815
Print Version: https://www.createspace.com/5051814
http://crimsoncloakpublishing.com/bill-hunt_2.html

http://crimsoncloakpublishing.com